Six Dead.
Don't go out at night.
Don't go out if you're pretty and blonde.
The what's your name killer strikes again.

Boken Girl Broken World

Eady H

Published by Eady H, 2024.

This is a work of fiction. Similarities to real people, places, or events are entirely coincidental.

BOKEN GIRL BROKEN WORLD

First edition. March 1, 2024.

Copyright © 2024 Eady H.

ISBN: 979-8224711840

Written by Eady H.

Cover by RuthAnna Evans

What's your name?

The whispered words pulled Bethany from sleep with a shiver despite the heat. She hadn't heard those words in months. She didn't really believe she'd heard them now, but her pounding heart told her otherwise. She pulled a prescription bottle from her pack and turned it over in her hands. Empty. Just like the last four times she'd tried to take them. And it would remain empty now that the world had ended.

No one believed her when she claimed the what's your name killer was stalking her. Everyone called her attention seeking. They sent her to therapy, but it hadn't helped. Now all of those non-believers were dead or undead.

Bethany tried to return to sleep, but the white noise of the zombies moans below her, and thoughts of the killer kept her awake. Odds were he was long dead. Just like everyone else. She finally slipped into a restless sleep and when she woke in the morning her eyes were gritty. She shifted in her hammock while she wiped her eyes. As she blinked them open, she saw angry scratches in the tree she was camping in. The words 'what's your name' were carved in the trunk facing her. Bethany glanced down at her hand and saw wood chips sticking out from under her chipped nails. The tips of her fingers were sore and raw.

She glanced from her hand back at the tree. The scratches were still there. Bethany shivered as the words danced before her eyes. Tears dripped down her face. Why would she have done this? How could she have done this. She reached again for her prescription bottle, but it was still empty. She curled her legs up to her chin and wrapped her arms around them. "It's all in your head. It's all in your head," she muttered. She'd dealt with the inevitable jaws of death for the last six months so why did the words what's your name still make her tremble like a leaf. The killer was long dead. She was alone. Minus the moaning undead below her.

When her tears finally subsided Bethany rolled up her hammock then climbed down from the tree. The zombies had started to scatter by the time she got her camp packed up. She'd discovered if you were quiet then they left you alone. But in the beginning, everyone had been screaming and there'd been a lot of looting, so the zombies had been in a frenzy.

Bethany's steps were slow as she worked at the splinters under her cracked nails. Her thoughts were on the words carved into the tree. Why had she done it and how did the action not wake her?

As she walked, she checked random mailboxes for letters. It made her feel less alone to read them. The mailboxes she found empty she left her own letters in for the old residents. It made her feel better. Like those people would come home and open it and it might make them smile to see someone had thought of them during such a shit time.

Bethany opened a mailbox to find a newspaper. The front-page article was about the 'what's your name killer.' She dropped it like it had burned her and it landed on the ground with a soft slap. The breeze flipped the pages as Bethany's eyes blurred with tears.

She felt dumb that this still affected her so strongly. It had been six months since the killer had targeted her. A fact no one else believed. And now the apocalypse swirled around her yet just the mention of the killer still made her bawl. Bethany turned and fled. The sound of her feet pounding the pavement drowned out the moaning of stray zombies wandering the neighborhood.

When her steps slowed, she was near a tall iron fence. She grabbed the bars in both hands and let the fence hold her up as she sucked in air. Snot dribbled down onto her lip, and she swiped at it then used the back of her hands to wipe her eyes. With her vision clear, she noticed she was in front of an insane asylum.

A dry laugh escaped her in a bark. If this had been six months ago, she might have eventually called this place home. She thought of the plain white strait jackets that sounded like a nice thing to try right about now so she wouldn't scratch what's your name in anything else. She thought of the meds for crazy people and that convinced her to push open the gate and walk toward the towering building made of stone with Gargoyles on the roof. Thin windows were covered by bars and barely let any natural light into the building. Bethany walked faster. She nearly ran up the steps and tugged on the door but found it locked. She rested her forehead against it and slammed her open palms on it while she screamed. Moaning came from behind her, but she didn't care she was drawing zombies to her. What good was it to be the lone person in this world. The door disappeared from under her palms, and she fell inside the building. Cool darkness wrapped around her as she heard the door slam shut.

"Girl what are you suicidal." a harsh whisper cut into her ears.

Bethany picked herself off the ground. She'd never considered herself suicidal but maybe she had just given up caring whether she lived or died. What was the use in living if she was crazy?

"Why'd you want in here so bad anyway?" the voice said.

"I want a straight-jacket and some medicine."

The voice laughed. "Straight jacket I can get you. Medicine not so much."

"Not regular medicine. I need antipsychotics."

Bethany felt a hand on her head stroking her hair. "Oh honey, you're not crazy, the dead are walking."

She slapped at the hand. "I'm not dumb."

A flashlight clicked on and shone in her face. "Didn't say you were. What's your name?"

The question echoed in her ears, and she froze. Tears started to leak from her eyes and her body trembled. It was insane to think this person was the killer.

"Okay, never seen such a visceral reaction to that question. Maybe you should see our resident shrink."

The person pointed the flashlight down and she finally got a look at a young man. His face was babyish and some of her tension eased. He motioned her to follow him deeper into the building and hesitantly she did. He led her past a tall set of windows, and she could see from the natural light. Her guide was slim and unnaturally well-groomed for the end of the world. Bethany was sure she looked a mess and self-consciously she smoothed her hair. She hadn't seen another living human since she'd gathered her nerve to leave her house and locked her undead parents inside.

The man led her to a room filled with couches, tables, books, and games. At the opposite end of the room there was a counter under a closed roll down gate. Bethany had seen a show that took place in an insane asylum once. Based on that she believed the medicine was kept behind that roll down gate.

He led her up to it and stopped. "The psychiatrist is in there."

"Uhm..."

"He locked himself in after a resident bit him. All the meds are with him. It's still cathartic to talk to him," he said as he gestured at a chair sitting next to the gate. "I'll give you some privacy."

He walked away and Bethany watched him go. She'd rather have the meds and the straight jacket. She'd talked to psychiatrists before. They all thought she was paranoid or lying about being stalked by the killer. Although now signs were pointing to paranoid. What were the odds he had lived through the rise of the dead. There were precious few people left.

Bethany sat in the chair and looked down at her feet. She could hear the psychiatrist moaning behind the door. She didn't even know what to say to him. But at least he couldn't tell her she was crazy. Tears smarted her eyes. The medicine she needed was right on the other side of that door. She stood and tried to find a way to raise the gate. The man returned and grabbed her arms.

"No. He must stay there. We need him."

Bethany didn't even try to fight. She sagged back into the chair and let her tears finally fall. She just wanted relief from her mind. She smacked her palms against the sides of her head.

"Do you know what it's like to be trapped in your own mind?" she sobbed looking up at him.

He looked down at her. "Yes, I do. That's why we need the psychiatrist. He helps. Trust me. I'm Jeremy by the way. But you can call me Remy."

She sniffed. "Bethany."

"You weren't really serious about the straight jacket, were you? I can tell you from personal experience they aren't any fun."

She shrugged. She thought she needed it to keep from harming herself, but she didn't suppose being in one around a stranger was safe. "Why do you stay here?"

"I don't stay here. I just sleep here."

"What's the difference?" she asked wiping her nose on her sleeve.

"I'm a street cleaner."

"You mean like a garbage man?"

"Eh . . . in this case it's more like a mortician. I put the undead to rest to make room for the living."

Roughly six months ago

The WYN killer gently pulled the lungs out on his sixth victim. A girl he believed was the sixth seal of Revelation. Each one an angelic being, he opened into a blood eagle and suspended above the floor. As he worked on her lungs, the body began to jerk, and he halted his movements. The girl was long dead, her mortal body unable to handle what he was putting it through to open the seal. He finished his work and rounded the still jerking body. The girls' eyes were open like he'd left them. And with her blood he'd drawn a six on her forehead and tears under her blue eyes. But now her mouth was open, and she acted like she saw him. She made biting motions in his direction and there was a low moaning in her throat. For a moment he watched his little angel try to get him then he turned and left the scene. There was one more seal to open and he had to finish his preparations.

Present

Bethany woke in her hammock in the tree she had hung it in the night prior. She'd chosen not to sleep in the insane asylum especially after Remy had introduced her to the rest of his group. There were three more men and a woman with pale blond hair and blue eyes. All of them committed to cleaning the streets. They seemed nice but she didn't know them, and they'd all admitted that the insane asylum had been home long before the end of the world. As she moved, she felt a shooting pain in her left arm and looked down. Her sleeve was rolled up and the letters WYN were cut into her flesh. She glanced at her right hand and found a bloody pocketknife. She recognized it as the one she'd picked up in her first days alone after the dead began to walk. Hot tears ran down her face for the second morning in a row. Why would she do that to herself? Why couldn't she remember doing it?

Bethany sat in her hammock, head hung down and let the tears soak her front. When her eyes had no more moisture to give, she scrubbed her shirt over her face and bandaged her arm before covering it with her sleeve. Better the others didn't see it.

When she felt ready to face them, she climbed down from the tree and entered the asylum. The girl who called herself Dutch was dancing down the hallway to no music and Bethany wondered why such a harmless pixie had been sent to live in the asylum. Dutch grabbed her as she passed and pulled her into the dance. Bethany tried to worm her way out of the embrace, but Dutch continued to pull her down the hallway in the dance. They waltzed into the community room that Remy had taken her to the day before. Bert, one of the other men was sitting in front of the prescription room talking through the door to the psychiatrist. Jake and Mike were playing foosball and Remy was not in the room. Dutch spun Bethany into a soft chair and continued dancing. Remy entered the room a few minutes later and approached her.

"Ready for your first day of street cleaning?" he asked.

"I don't really think I can." Bethany had never killed anything before. The thought of it made her insides shake.

"It's just like when you've done it for self-defense. Only this is to save others."

"I've never had to kill one in self-defense." She'd never had a need to. She'd always been alone. Always been quiet.

"Never? And it's not killing. It's releasing the soul. It's actually very beautiful. I love watching their spirit come unstuck from the rotting corpse. Very therapeutic."

Bethany looked at him confused. How did one see a spirit?

"Come on, I'll show you," Remy said as he motioned her to follow him.

Bethany looked around at the others who were ignoring them before getting up to follow him from the asylum. He grabbed a sharpened stick from next to the door and the two of them wandered down the street until they came across a zombie shambling down the sidewalk. It was on the opposite side of the street and facing them. Bethany assumed they would walk up and kill it with no problems, but it changed direction and lurched across the street toward them even though they had been silent. Remy raised the stick and moved toward it at a quicker pace. He stabbed it through the eye into the brain and the zombie stopped mid step. He moved his gaze above its head and looked up into the sky.

"Did you see it?" he asked with a smile.

Bethany assumed he thought he'd seen its ghost rise above it though she hadn't seen anything. But a part of her was scared to admit that to him. She didn't know how he'd react. "Yep," she said and nodded for emphasis. Maybe he had a gift she didn't. Who knew maybe the ghosts of all the people were trapped until they were let out. Who was she to doubt it? Until six months ago people laughed at the idea of zombies. Most of them were dead now and she was determined not to deny something she could neither prove nor disprove.

"It's great work we're doing," he said excitedly. "Won't you join us? We'll be heroes to the new world."

Bethany didn't want to be heroic. She just wanted to be sane. "Sure." What else was she going to do with her time? So far, she'd just been existing. This seemed to be living.

For the rest of the day, she helped Remy clean the street. He was exuberant every time they liberated a soul as he called it. But she felt nothing. If this was living, she didn't feel alive. She felt dirty. In the literal sense. She was covered in clotted blood and gore that exploded out of some of the more decomposed zombies. Remy encouraged her to leave the bodies where they fell. Bert, Jack, and Mike cleaned up the mess behind them. Dutch danced among the dead-dead, the undead, and the living. Bethany wished she could get lost in the song with the pixie. Then maybe she might feel. But all she was, was hollow. How anyone found this task fulfilling was beyond her.

Before the zombie apocalypse she'd had dreams. Hopes. Goals. She'd wanted to go to college. Maybe travel abroad before settling down. Now all of that was gone. Travelling abroad would never happen now no matter how much street cleaning was done. Granted her life had begun to spiral when she realized she was being stalked by the WYN killer. Her schoolwork had suffered first followed by her social life. Everyone thought she was attention seeking. What Bethany really heard was she wasn't special enough to be the victim of a serial murderer. Not with her muddy blond hair when the other six girls had lighter blond hair. Poor Bethany so unremarkable she had to make up being stalked by a serial killer so people would pay attention to her.

As evening approached the street cleaners led her back to the asylum where she was able to take a shower since the asylum had solar panel power. She made sure to wash any gore away from her arm wound. That night she once again slept in her hammock in the tree. Away from the others she was more comfortable. She finally unwound the bandage on her arm so it could get some air, but she couldn't bring herself to look at it.

The next morning when she woke, her forehead stung. Bethany pulled the little compact mirror she carried out of her bag. She only looked in it when she was overcome by loneliness. Now she used it to inspect her forehead. She found a crudely carved number seven in her forehead, now crusted in blood and the mirror shook in her hand. She licked her fingertips and swiped at the blood, but the carving stayed. Once more her eyes smarted, with tears but this time she tried to keep them in. The effort burned her chest and she sniffed.

What the hell was wrong with her? What sort of a person did these things to themselves?

Bethany dug through her bag until she found a winter hat which she pulled down on her head far enough to cover the number then she wrapped up her arm and once more covered it with a sleeve. With a deep breath she climbed down from the tree and met up with the street cleaners for another day of releasing souls. Today she tried to be more like Dutch and leave the soul freeing to Remy. Bethany went back to her old habit of checking mailboxes instead. If the pixie could dance, she could read. Let the men be heroic.

Remy watched through a window as Bethany climbed up into the tree outside the asylum. He understood why she slept out there. In this new world, not everyone kept their humanity. Those people were worse than the undead. As the sun descended Remy walked out of the building and through the front gate. This was his favorite time of day. The undead moved less and he was freer to just be. During the day he felt the pressure of his mission to free the spirits of the undead. He couldn't imagine what it must be like to be trapped in a rotting body. He often wondered if they could smell their own decomposition.

This time of day also helped him to see the free souls. They were clearer at twilight. As he walked among them, they smiled and nodded, and he felt at peace. He was doing a good thing. Remy was going to save the world one freed soul at a time. When the sun had disappeared completely, he returned to the asylum and stood under the tree Bethany slept in. He could hear her soft snore from the ground. He knew she hadn't believed him about the spirits. And she was disgusted by killing. But he was going to make her see. He was a good man.

Days turned into weeks and Bethany went out every day with Remy and the street cleaners. While he saved his spirits, she left messages to the old tenants and maybe one day the new ones. Eventually she recognized that she was wandering her old neighborhood, and she approached her street. She could at least release her parents' spirits. Maybe that would help her get past her disgust at what Remy was doing. As she walked down her old street, she noticed that all of the mailboxes had their red flags up and they hadn't been up when she'd locked her parents in the house and fled. Curiously she checked each mailbox and found a slip of paper that said, 'what's your name?'

Each time she opened a mailbox and pulled the letter out, her hands shook, and she dropped the paper letting the breeze carry it away. The terrifying confetti skipped down the street and caught in bushes. Despite her terror she checked each box before coming to stand in front of her old home. The door hung open swaying in the wind. When she'd left the door had been shut firmly behind her. There hadn't been a need to lock it. Zombies couldn't turn the door handles. She approached the open door cautiously and poked her head inside.

"Mom, dad," she called and listened to her shaky voice echo through the house. Neither of them shambled forward looking for a meal so she stepped inside and went room to room. The rest of the house was as she had left it. There were no blood stains indicating her parents had caught a human entering the dwelling. Bethany climbed the stairs and entered her own bedroom. The stain on the wall above her bed was still there. She'd tried to scrub off the 'what's your name' that had been painted on there. With what she was unsure because it hadn't come all the way off. The ghost of the letters still taunted her. Words everyone else said she had written herself. And now she was beginning to suspect they were right. If she could self-harm in her sleep, maybe she had painted the words on the wall. Maybe she was unremarkable and wanted attention. Although who was there to give it now. Her parents were undead and so were her friends. She'd checked. And some small part of her was a little happy they were. She'd seen it as karma for doubting her.

Bethany stepped back out of her bedroom and noticed the ladder to the attic was down. She knew she hadn't pulled it down before she'd left. She pulled a flashlight from her bag and stepped under the opening in the ceiling.

"Hello," she called up. "Mom, dad, some stranger hiding from the undead."

No one answered her. Bethany ascended the ladder into the attic and shone her flashlight around. What she saw made her insides churn. Light came in from one window and highlighted a wall filled with pictures of her. Pictures taken from a distance, and she'd had no idea they were taken. In another corner of the attic, she found a bed.

She dropped to her knees and the flashlight slid from her fingers. She'd been right. The killer had been stalking her. And he'd been living right above her the whole time.

Roughly six months ago

Bethany opened her locker and a picture fluttered out. She bent down to retrieve it and saw it was a picture of her taken from a distance. She'd never seen it before. In red letters across the picture were the words 'what's your name.' She stared at it confused. She'd heard of the killer just like everyone else, but she couldn't fathom why someone would put the picture in her locker. On her forehead in the picture was the number 7. That also confused her. The killer had only killed five victims.

Students began running down the hall toward the cafeteria. She slammed her locker and followed them to see what was up. The tv's in the room were displaying a news segment. It showed officers approaching what looked like one of the WYN killers' victims. But she appeared alive. She bit at the approaching officers and the click of her teeth echoed. The victim had a number 6 on her forehead. Bethany looked down at the photo in her hand and it shook. She pulled her phone from her pocket and called her mom.

Present day

Bethany dreamed she was back in her school holding the picture that marked her as a victim of WYN. A police officer stood next to her. "Only your fingerprints are on the picture. Why did you make this story up? The WYN victims are blonde."

"I am blonde."

The officer laughed at her. "You're damn near a brunette."

"He's stalking me. Please you have to believe me."

The officer only laughed.

Bethany woke with a start and saw Remy sitting on the branch across from her hammock. "What are you doing?"

"You need to come inside."

"Why?"

"Just come. Please."

Remy dropped down out of the tree and disappeared in the dark. His voice had sounded urgent, so she climbed groggily from her hammock and went into the asylum. Remy hadn't waited on her, so she went to the community room where she imagined he was. Remy, Bert, Mike, and Jake were gathered around something in the corner of the room. Bethany approached them and heard something from where they were looking. The men parted and she saw Dutch. Her ribs and lungs had been pulled out of her back and she looked just like the WYN killer's victims. There was no number on her head though. Bethany began to tremble, and her vision clouded with tears. Dutch bit and snapped at them.

"Release her spirit," Remy said.

Bethany shook her head. On the floor in front of Dutch the words 'what's your name' had been written in Dutch's blood.

"What's that on your arm?" Bert asked. "And your forehead?"

Bethany slid her hand over her arm. "Nothing." She hadn't had time to cover her arm or her forehead before she'd come in. Not that she'd been awake enough to even think about it.

"It looks like the same words that are painted in front of Dutch."

"And her hands are red," Mike said pointing at them.

Bethany turned and fled into the night. She didn't bother to fetch her things from the tree, she just ran. Harming herself in her sleep was one thing. Murdering an innocent girl was another. How could she have done that? She'd started to think her mind was healing. For weeks she hadn't done anything to herself. She started to let the others in. Bethany had even thought about moving out of her tree and into the asylum with them. Now she was bereft again. Alone and without her supplies.

She ran until her sides ached and she could scarcely breathe. When she stopped, she was standing in front of a church. She heard a voice inside and wrestled with herself about going in. But she knew she needed help. She'd killed in the exact way she'd feared dying. She eased the door open and entered. Candles lit the sanctuary in a soft glow. Zombies were sitting in the pews and there was a man at the pulpit dressed like a priest. Bethany slipped into an empty pew at the back, a little curious and a little in need of saving.

"Behold yourselves sinners. See your sin on your disgusting flesh," the priest yelled into the room.

The zombies tried to stand at the commotion and Bethany heard chains rattle holding them in their pews.

"Christ conquered death when he rose from the grave. And you have the gall to sit here and mock him with your rotting flesh after you crawled from the grave like you were the messiah himself. Repent."

The zombies were moaning, and the sound filled the sanctuary. The priest took it as a sign of their willingness to welcome Christ. He began to walk around the room and make the sign of the cross on each zombies' forehead. When he got to Bethany he paused.

"You're not a sinner," he said.

Tears rolled down Bethany's cheeks. "Oh, but I am father."

He took her hands and showed them to her. "You can see sin on the flesh."

Bethany turned her arm so he could see the letters carved into her arm then withdrew her hand and pointed at her forehead. The priest smoothed his thumb over the 7.

"This is a holy number. A sign of perfection," he said.

Bethany shook her head unable to believe that. She'd cut letters and numbers into herself. She'd murdered an innocent girl. She needed help.

"You are holy, divine. And you have been sent here in our species hour of need."

"What do you mean?"

"The sinners have overrun the world. God has called us to start over. To be fruitful and multiply."

"Me and you?" Bethany asked suddenly disgusted. The priest was old enough to be her father, perhaps older. She'd never been a good judge of age.

The priest gave a small chuckle. "I'm flattered, but no. A young man just recently found himself on this threshold as well. A new Adam and Eve."

"I'm not sure I'm comfortable with this," Bethany said. "I'm only seventeen."

"Oh, my dear. Age is simply a number when you've been chosen by God. Do you know how old Abraham was when he fathered children?"

"Okay but I'm not sure I want to bring a child into this shit show of a world. Pardon my language father."

The priest gave a tight-lipped smile. "Now is when we need children the most. How will we carry on if we don't procreate?"

"Um, we're back to the we that makes me uncomfortable."

"Come my little Eve. Let us meet your Adam," the priest said as he pulled her to her feet.

Unsure how to get out of this awkward situation she followed him. Where else did she have to go? He led her past the pews and behind the pulpit where there was a door. On the other side was a small room with a tub. A man sat on the floor in front of it.

"Adam, this is your Eve," the priest said. "I'll leave you two to get acquainted. No consummating until I perform your baptisms. Now if you'll excuse me, I have more souls to save."

"Who the fuck is Adam," the guy asked.

"Language, you're in the house of the lord."

"He ain't my lord bro."

"He is lord of all, Adam. We'll speak of this when I'm done with my sermon."

The priest shut the door and Bethany was left alone with the man she was supposed to repopulate the earth with. He looked like he worshipped Satan not Jesus. She regretted trying to find peace in the church. Her family had never been religious. But she was desperate to feel like she might be forgiven on some level for what she had done. She'd become what she feared. A murderer.

"Since my name isn't Adam, I imagine you're not Eve," the guy said. "I'm Dean."

"Bethany. Look um . . ."

"You don't have to worry. I'm gay. I'm not reproducing shit."

"Oh, thank God, or the devil, whatever you're into."

"I don't think either exists."

Bethany sat down next to him. "What do we do now?"

"I say we get the hell out of here."

"There's nowhere to go," Bethany said. She couldn't go back to where she'd come from even though all of her supplies were there. She had nothing and no one. And she wasn't even sure she should be around other people now that she was a murderer. What if she had a taste for it now.

"Anywhere. The continent is our oyster. You really wanna stay here and be treated like a cow?"

No, she didn't, but she was scared to be around others. "I'll leave the building with you, because I think its going to take both of us to get past him. But then I'm going my own way."

"Is it cause I'm gay?"

"What? No. I just . . . I'm just better off on my own and other people are better off away from me. Why would you think it's cause you're gay."

"We're in the bible belt bro."

"I'm not religious. Just really fucked up."

"Aren't all of us these days. The dead are walking. We've all lost people and had to kill to survive."

"It wasn't always to survive."

"I'm not here to judge you. But you said it yourself. We're stronger together and not just against the zealot priest. Humans are pack animals. We need others to be sane. And whatever you've done, it's in the past."

"It's not even been two hours."

He let out a nervous laugh. "Look. I'm on my own. I've been on my own for a long time. And I'm tired. Tired of looking over my shoulder and not sleeping. And I'm sensing you're the same. I don't need to know all of your secrets and I won't tell you mine. But can we at least form a partnership where we keep each other alive. Above all else."

Bethany thought about it for a moment. She was lonely. She'd enjoyed living around the street cleaners. But now she had ruined that. But Dean was alone. And not a blond woman. Perhaps she wouldn't murder him since he didn't look like a WYN victim. "Okay. How do we get out of this church?"

Dean smiled. "That's easy. Follow my lead." Dean stood, took Bethany's hand and pulled her to her feet, but he didn't let go of her. Dean led Bethany out of the small room and up behind the priest. He was really giving the zombies a hellfire and brimstone sermon.

"Father." He whispered in between words.

The priest paused mid-sentence and turned toward them. "Yes?"

"Uh, Eve and I cannot procreate here. We must find the new Eden. There we will restart the human race."

Bethany expected the priest to refuse, but he smiled really big.

"That's a great idea," he said. "Go with god."

"You as well," Dean said and led Bethany outside.

"Wow that was really fucking easy. How did you know that would work?"

"He's a religious zealot and I was raised among them. Not rocket science," Dean said as he let go of her hand.

"I'm sorry that must have been rough." Bethany couldn't even imagine growing up with religion, let alone among people like the priest. And it must have been worse for him because he was gay. She, like him had wanted to live her life for herself, not some invisible god who may not exist. It wasn't like she was a bad person. And she didn't think Dean was either. "Also, can we uh take the path that doesn't go near the insane asylum."

"Not gonna ask, but god I want to."

"I just . . ." tears smarted her eyes again. "I can't talk about it." She sniffed and turned her head away.

"You don't have to share anything you don't want to."

Bethany nodded and wiped her eyes. She wasn't sure she'd ever share what the past few weeks had been for her. She knew if she told Dean he would probably leave. And she knew that's what was best. What was safe. But she couldn't bring herself to do it. Something stopped her from withdrawing and becoming solo again. She couldn't remember the last time she had had a friend. Most of hers had bailed on her when they called her a liar for claiming the WYN killer was stalking her. And then everyone she presumed had died though she'd kept to herself in an attempt to keep herself safe from other people so she couldn't say for certain.

"How old are you?" Dean asked.

"Seventeen."

"Oh, to be seventeen again. Not that I'd go back if I had the chance. Your twenties are where it's at. Especially, your late twenties. It's when you start to like yourself because you've found the person you want to be."

"I guess I won't really know what that's like. Now there is only the you that is capable of surviving."

"Not true babe. Life is what you make it, not just what you do to survive."

Bethany had been just surviving for longer than she cared to admit. From the moment the picture of her had fallen out of her locker with the words 'what's your name' on it she'd been in survival mode. "What's the point? We're all on borrowed time."

"Is it fun living like that?"

"Fun?"

"When was the last time you had fun?"

"Six months before the world fully ended."

"Very specific but okay. Let's have some fun."

"How does one have fun in the apocalypse?" Everything was gone and there was no power.

"Such a Debbie downer this one. The mall still stands. Doesn't every seventeen-year-old girl love to shop?"

Bethany gave him a small smile. When she had friends, she loved the mall. "Okay."

Dean and Bethany walked the rest of the way to the mall in a comfortable silence. His presence put Bethany at ease, and she hadn't felt that way in months.

"We should stick together inside. No telling how many zombies are in there."

Bethany shrugged. She'd never had any problems with the zombies. They'd never paid her any attention unless she made loud noises, but she'd noticed while with the street cleaners that the zombies were drawn to them. "The mall is empty. Some people I know are cleaning the streets of zombies and I saw them empty the mall."

"Sweet."

The two of them entered the pitch-black structure. Despite the apocalypse, Bethany found it eerily quiet. "Can we maybe wait till morning to have some fun?"

"Good idea. Let's find a place to bunk down for the night. Maybe after our shopping spree we can find a roller rink."

That night Dean and Bethany slept in a closet. Dean thought if they were in a closed space nothing could sneak up on them. The remainder of their night passed uncomfortably. When the first rays of light began to light up the building they crawled from their cramped bedroom. Bethany led Dean to the food court, and they scrounged some food.

Dean agreed to part ways when Bethany pointed out they had completely different styles despite his saying girlfriends stick together. He went to find a hot topic and she went in search of a dress shop. She was tired of practical apocalyptic wear. She wanted to feel pretty, even if no one else thought she was. It had really stung when her friends said she wasn't pretty enough to have caught the WYN killers' eye. That she was plain at best. She'd been hoping to reinvent her look in college, but now that dream was gone.

Bethany located one of those stores that had two levels and sold makeup as well as clothing. First, she found a large purse like bag and tossed in some makeup before scouring the full racks. She was glad Dean had gone to a different store. She was self-conscious about trying on clothes in front of other people. When her arms were loaded, she went to a fitting room and tried them on. One by one she cast the items aside not liking what she saw in the mirror.

Bethany had been modestly plump six months ago, now her frame seemed more skeletal. Probably because food was hard to come by. A gnawing hunger always seemed to persist. She left the last item on, a long red dress with a slit up the leg to the hip. It wasn't flattering on her new frame, but it was clean, unlike her own clothes. Bethany sat on the floor in front of the mirror and attempted to use makeup to look better.

As she was finishing up, she heard a voice out in the store. "Coming Dean." She didn't want him to worry. Bethany shoved the clothes into the bag. Odds are she wouldn't see a mirror again for a long time and she needed clothing. Next, she'd look into shoes.

She ambled out of the fitting room area and expected Dean to tease her about the dress in a good-natured way. But she didn't find Dean. Instead, she found three strange men. She tried to backtrack quietly, but they caught sight of her.

"Look what we have here."

"It's like she got all dressed up for us."

Her hands twitched nervously, and she gripped her bag tighter. "No actually this is for my boyfriend. Have you seen him? Goth looking guy."

"A girl that looks like you with a goth?" the men laughed.

"Well, it's the uh end of the world and the pickings are slim you know."

"I'd say your options have widened."

"Lucky you."

"I mean its unlucky for you because there is only one of me and now a total of four men."

"We don't mind sharing."

Bethany swallowed hard. These men gave off a threatening air. And she was at a bit of a disadvantage. She was barefoot and wearing this stupid dress. God why did Dean suggest shopping.

Bethany dropped the bag and sprinted away from the men. If she could just make it to hot topic, she might have a chance. She felt something snag the dress from behind and she screamed until her throat hurt. She was jerked backward and landed hard on her back. One of the men stood over her with a leering grin.

"I caught you, so I get to go first."

She tried to scuttle backward but he climbed on top of her and pinned her to the floor. His hand slid up her leg which was hanging out of the slit in her dress. She squirmed underneath him and he grabbed her head then slammed it into the floor until she saw stars. She felt his weight leave her before she passed out completely.

When Bethany woke, she was surrounded by darkness, and she started to panic. She felt a hand in hers holding on tight.

"Shh Bethany you're safe," Dean said.

"Where am I? Did he? No don't tell me."

"No, he didn't. I apologize for agreeing to leave you alone. The world isn't safe."

"What happened? I blacked out."

"While I was at hot topic, I ran into some people who were part of a group travelling to an underground city. I was discussing joining them when I heard you scream. We ran to find you and I saw that guy sitting on top of you and I tackled him. The group took him and the other two which they caught, and they punished them. Don't ask how."

"Why do I feel motion?"

"I joined their caravan. If you want out, we can get off at the next town we come across. But this underground city might be our best chance at survival. Things are getting crazier every day. Also, if anyone asks, I told them you're my little sister."

"I will agree to going to this city on one condition. Every night when I go to bed, I want you to tie me up. You don't get to ask why. I just need you to do it."

"That's a little kinky sister."

Bethany laughed. Dean really did feel like a brother in the moment. His teasing was lighthearted, and it made her feel human again. "How long is this trip supposed to be?"

"Couple of days. I guess they have been in contact with people who are on the way, and they've been stopping and picking them up as they go. They only stopped at the mall to find extra supplies. Instead, they got us."

It took them three days to get where they were going, stopping periodically to pick up other people or to scrounge for supplies. Bethany kept to herself, but Dean seemed to come alive among the people in the bus they rode in. She felt like she was holding him back. But he didn't seem to mind. Dean checked on her frequently and he always looked a little sad when he looked at her. She knew he still felt bad for what had happened at the mall, but it hadn't been his fault.

Bethany found herself in awe of her first look at the city. Two gigantic doors were set in a cliff face. They slid open as the caravan approached. The entire caravan could have driven inside at once and there would have still been room between them and the doors. Once they were all inside the doors slid closed silently behind them. The absence of the sun was the first thing Bethany noticed. All of the light now was white artificial light. Somehow the city still had power and Bethany heard people murmuring around her about real hot showers.

Bethany seemed to be the only one uneasy since the doors closed behind them. The absence of light wasn't the only thing that caused her concern. She was just as worried she'd kill someone else without knowing.

Dean took her hand and squeezed, and she gave him a grateful smile. Her adopted brother would tie her up at night. She would contain the monster she had become. She would have a normal life again. Here she could be a teenager again.

A man met them inside the doors and gestured for them to stop their vehicles. "Friends, you no longer need your vehicles. Here we go everywhere on foot. If you would please form single file lines in front of my fellow citizens here. You're going to be sorted based on skills. Once a job has been assigned to you then you will get a rooming assignment."

The people started murmuring, a swell of voices filling the room at once and sweeping over them like a tide. They sounded angry and frustrated.

The man held his hands up. "Friends, friends. We are in no way attempting to separate anyone. Children will still be with their parents and couples will be housed together. But housing assignments are based on jobs. We expend less energy if we're housed by our area of work."

There were still suspicious murmurs from the crowd of people. Dean weaved around them and pulled Bethany with him to the front. He led her to one of the sorting people. "I'm Dean, this is my underage sister Bethany. I was working on a bachelors in botany when the world ended. I am also handy with a hammer and nails."

The woman smiled at him. "Welcome to new hope. We do have an opening in the gardens. How old is Bethany?"

"I'm seventeen."

The woman smiled again. "Great age. You'll be allowed to pick a field to apprentice in. You may try out several until you find the right fit. Your housing will be on level four A, near the gardens. Here are key cards for your room. It also gives you access to the elevator. Please attach your thumb prints to your room once you access it. Someone will be by later to give you a tour and a work schedule."

Dean took the keys then led Bethany past the line of assignees. A set of Elevators were behind the line, and he slid the card opening an elevator. The two of them stepped on and watched the crowd of people slowly approach the citizens of new hope to receive job and housing assignments. It seemed as good as this deal was, trust was hard to come by for people who had witnessed the worst and survived.

"You still feel okay about this?" Dean asked.

"I mean . . . what else do we do?"

"I don't know but if you have second thoughts we can go back up, take a vehicle and leave."

Bethany sighed. She had so many thoughts about this new living situation. Was it safe? Who were these people? Why were they being so nice? And didn't she owe it to Dean to try and make this work? He seemed happier since he was around people. "We can try it. Might be good."

"Well, it is called new hope," he said with a laugh. "Corny motherfuckers."

Bethany joined in his laugh. It was a dumb name. "Thank you, by the way. For keeping us together."

"For sure little sister."

The elevator stopped and the door slid open to reveal a cavernous area. Above them walkways stretched across the space to and from doorways on other floors. This level had a rock floor and sloped further underground. Signs with room numbers were posted on the walls with arrows. Dean followed the arrows to their room and slid a key letting them in. The inside looked remarkably like a hotel room. It had two twin beds and its own bathroom.

"Which bed do you want?" Dean asked.

"I don't think it matters. Not like there's a view from a window."

Dean flopped onto the nearest bed. "I know. When the sun disappeared, I was instantly sadder."

"Maybe working in the gardens will help you some," Bethany said as she set her bag of meager belongings down on her bed.

"It might help you too. Maybe you should do your apprenticeship in the garden."

Bethany gave a half-hearted shrug. "I don't know what I want to do." She'd originally wanted to go into medicine but footage of the WYN victims had made her gag, so she'd been rethinking her life when she'd begun to be stalked by the killer. After that she hadn't thought of much else besides her impending death.

"You've got time to figure it out kiddo. Let's see what other jobs they even have around this joint. Ah god a joint. What I wouldn't do for one of those. Is it too much to hope they grow weed in the garden?"

"Probably. What's it like?"

"Being high? Like your whole body is floating. It's even better than being drunk."

"Never been that either."

"Oh my god girl. You're a goody two-shoes. I'm going to change that."

"What the hell, might as well try some new things."

"You bet your ass big brother is going to show you how to be bad."

Three hours later someone knocked on their door. Dean opened it to admit a man about his age. The man smiled at both of them as he entered.

"I'm Kevin. Nice to meet you both."

"I'm Dean and this is my sister Bethany."

"Welcome to New Hope. I'm going to steal Dean for a bit and show him around the garden. After that we'll swing by the room to get you and I'll show you guys around. Sound good?"

"Sure," Bethany said.

"I'll be right back," Dean said. "Okay."

Bethany nodded and smiled. Dean followed Kevin out of the room. The minute the door shut Bethany let her smile slip. She was alone in a strange place for the first time in a long time. Suddenly the room felt too small. She'd thought she'd thrived by herself, but in the last several days she'd grown accustomed to Dean's presence. He was like a safety blanket and over the last three hours she'd come to know him like a friend.

Bethany sat on her bed and drew her knees up to her chin. She was worried moving underground would cause her to become a monster once more. And what if she couldn't find an apprenticeship that she liked. Would they separate her from Dean and kick her out?

An hour later Dean and Kevin returned to the room and Bethany followed them back out to get a tour of their new home. Kevin showed them the dining area, laundry, a place to find new clothes and bathroom supplies. There was even a library, a bowling alley, skating rink, a school for the younger kids, and a brewery. New Hope had everything people needed to not just survive, but live full lives. There was a sign up hanging near the dining area where classes were advertised if someone had a hankering to learn something new.

After the tour they grabbed lunch with Kevin. Bethany noticed how his attention had stayed on Dean the entire time, which she thought was cute. Dean seemed just as smitten as Kevin. This new world was lonely and any sense of being together was a cherished thing. She found she kind of envied their quick bond, she'd been estranged from other people since she'd found the picture of herself staged in her locker.

"Hey how about you guys come to a party tonight. It's going to be awesome and will give you a chance to meet people," Kevin said.

"What kind of party?" Dean asked.

"Does it matter?" Bethany asked. "Didn't you just tell me the other day we needed to have more fun?"

Dean laughed. "I just want to know what the vibe is before I get there."

"It's more of a rave. A couple of guys I'm friends with were in a garage band and they're putting on a show. Plus, one of them is also a chemist and he makes his own LSD which makes living below ground tolerable."

"And the leaders of this place are okay with that?" Bethany asked suddenly, worried about being kicked out or locked up.

Kevin laughed. "You were not kidding when you said she was a good kid."

"No, I was not. Our mother," Dean tutted. "Very strict. She's very lucky she has such a cool older brother."

"As long as everyone reports for their work shifts, they pretty much turn a blind eye to everything but murder and rape. Speaking of psychologically damaged people, now would probably be a good time to mention everyone has to visit the psychologist before they are cleared for work or apprenticeship."

That news settled like a stone in her stomach. She'd been sent to a psychiatrist before. The school had suggested it to her parents after the photo incident. She'd ended up on antipsychotics.

Dean shrugged like it was no big deal. "Point the way."

Kevin led them to the psychologist's office and Dean went first. Bethany sat in the waiting area picking at her fingernails and biting them.

"Calm down Bethany. It's just routine to make sure you're not dangerous."

Bethany began to sweat and fidget in her seat. When it was her turn, she could hardly stand and make herself walk into the office. She heard the snick of the door closing and it made her jump. The psychologist walked around her and took his seat.

"Why don't you sit down Bethany, and we'll get started. I'm Dr. Phil."

Bethany's gaze snapped to him and she started to smile. "Seriously that's your name?"

"Yes, it is," he said picking up his notebook. "Why don't you tell me a little about yourself. Dean didn't have too much to say about you."

She almost asked why he would, but remembered they were masquerading as siblings. "Uh, I'm seventeen. I'm an honor student. Well, I guess was an honor student. Both of my parents were victims of the zombie virus. Not really sure about the status of anyone else I knew."

"Why do I make you nervous, Bethany?"

"Um . . . because you have the power to kick me out of this place."

"Only in extreme cases is someone removed from the community. I'm here to help you transition back into society. I only want to help."

Bethany licked her lips and stared at him. She didn't know if she could trust him with the burdens inside her.

"Can you tell me about the marks on your forehead and arm. Who did them to you, and the impact it has made on you."

"I," she whispered then cleared her throat. "I did them."

"Why?"

"I don't know. I was asleep and I woke up and they were there."

"I find it hard to believe you did them then. Did Dean or another member of the group you were with assault you in any way."

Bethany started crying. "I was alone when I woke up and found these marks. And I know I did it, because I was supposed to be the seventh victim of the what's your name killer." Bethany scratched her forehead and forearm.

"I see," Dr. Phil leaned forward. "How do you know that?"

"The day they found the sixth victim I found a picture in my locker of me taken from far away and the words what's your name were written on it."

Roughly six months ago

Bethany sat in the principal's office with her parents, the picture on his desk. The principal sat leaning back in his chair, fingers steepled on his portly stomach staring at her.

"Principal Dixon, Bethany hasn't been in any trouble before. She's an A student. Surely this is some kid pulling a prank."

"The police came and fingerprinted the photo. The only prints are hers," Principal Dixon said.

"Well as she stated she picked it up off the floor. Hence her fingerprints. It's not unheard of for someone to wear gloves when they perpetrate a crime."

"No crime has been committed Mr. Clark. Simply a young girl's cry for attention."

"I didn't do it," Bethany said.

"Why are you questioning her word but not the word of the other students you interviewed?"

"How would one of them get into her locker?" the principal asked.

"Bethany please wait outside," her father said.

Bethany slipped out of the office and sat in a chair outside. She could hear the conversation heat up and she was fighting back tears. She rested her elbows on her knees and tried not to listen. Bethany's best friend entered the room and sat next to her smirking at Bethany.

"Guess Principal Dixon saw through your lies."

Bethany sat up like she'd been slapped. "My lies?"

"Give it up babe, you're not pretty enough to be the victim of a serial killer."

"Whawhat?"

"I mean don't get me wrong. You're pretty, just not that pretty."

Bethany shot to her feet and slapped her friend in the face, anger and shame burning her.

"Principal Dixon, Bethany hit me," she wailed.

Bethany's father and Principal Dixon came out of the office and saw the red mark on her face.

"Bethany what is the meaning of this?" her father asked.

"She was being an ass."

"Language," the principal said.

"All I did was try to talk some sense into her," her friend said. "These lies are not a good look."

"I didn't lie. Why doesn't anyone believe me?"

"Mr. Clark I'm urging you to get her help. I won't have these theatrics in my school. And she's suspended for the rest of the week for attacking a fellow student."

"Fuck you principal Dixon," Bethany screamed before running out of the office.

Present Day

Dean pulled clothes out of his bag and held them up for Bethany to see. "What should I wear?"

Bethany lay on her bed on her stomach watching Dean with amusement. "I'm sure Kevin will love anything you choose."

"You think? My god girl he was soo cute."

Bethany giggled. It had been so long since she'd talked boys with a friend. Everything here felt blissfully normal, and it made her giddy. Being a teenager for this one moment helped to overshadow her conversation with the psychologist. She hadn't wanted to, but she'd told him about the WYN killer and the events leading up to the end of the world in her own personal hell.

After choosing an outfit Dean went in the bathroom to take a shower and clean up. While he showered Bethany took out her own meager belongings. Dean had found the bag she'd filled with clothes in the mall and grabbed it when they carried her out and joined the caravan. She selected an outfit and waited her turn for the shower.

When both of them were ready they went to the dining area where they had agreed to meet Kevin. He was waiting for them, and he smiled when he saw them approach.

"I'm so glad you guys are coming."

"We're happy to be out," Dean said. "I've missed parties."

"There is no shortage of parties here," Kevin said leading them deeper into the underground town. Soon the harsh artificial lighting fell behind them and they left the carefully crafted living space of the underground town. The ground became uneven, and the space grew darker.

"Grab hands," Kevin said.

Dean, who was in the middle, took both of their hands and the group continued into the dark. Soon a soft glow appeared ahead of them and lessened the deep dark they were walking through. Music pumped through the cavern and Kevin tugged them along faster. They left the dark and entered a cavern lit with flashing party lights. A band stood on a makeshift stage deep in a song. Bodies pulsed in front of them to the beat.

Kevin led them to the tables set up along the wall and grabbed some cups that contained liquid and passed them out. Dean and Kevin took drinks out of their cups and Bethany looked at hers suspiciously. Dean nudged her arm and she looked at him.

"No one is going to make you do something you don't want to or don't feel safe doing, but you're safe with me. I won't let anything happen to you," Dean said.

Bethany smiled at him gratefully and took a drink. The contents were fruity but burned a little going down. Altogether it wasn't terrible, and she took some more sips. Her body started to buzz, and she felt calmer than she had in a long time. The alcohol coupled with the music made her body feel alive and she moved closer to the stage and began to dance.

Every burden she'd carried the last six months slipped away and her mind felt light. She drank and danced, losing herself in the moment. Time lost meaning and she lost herself. The careful, straight A student that always did what was expected and never lived on the edge slipped away. All that was left was the music and the buzz in her veins.

"What's your name?"

The whispered words made her halt mid dance and her eyes shot open. She spun and looked around but everyone else was still dancing. The words had been a whisper across her skin. Her stomach roiled and she moved off the dance floor and put her back up against the rough wall. Her heart pounded against her ribs, and she took huge gulping breaths. Her buzz was word off and now she just felt sick.

"Hey, you, okay?"

Bethany turned her head to look at the person who spoke to her. A girl her age leaned against the wall next to her, long blond hair hanging down her back.

"Yeah," Bethany gasped out.

"Woah wicked body marks. What does the seven stand for?"

"I'd rather not talk about it," Bethany said.

The girl shrugged. "Fair enough. My name's Jennifer."

"Bethany."

"You're new."

"I guess I am." Bethany had always feared being the new girl. They were always outcasts, but she'd become an outcast anyway.

"Wana do some LSD? It's a way better high than what's in those cups."

That was all the prodding Bethany needed. She wanted that free feeling once more. To forget what it was like to be hunted by a man and then her own mind. She had nothing to fear. WYN was dead right. Or perhaps undead. And she'd walked right past him on the street and never known. "Fuck it yeah I want some."

Jennifer handed her a small square of paper. "Stick this under your tongue."

Bethany did as she was instructed while Jennifer did the same. After that they got more drinks and leaned back against the wall. Bethany sipped her drink and people watched while she waited on the LSD to kick in.

"You have anyone left?" Jennifer asked,

"My brother Dean, he's . . ." Bethany looked around until she found him. "Uh he's over there making out with a guy named Kevin."

Jennifer looked where she was pointing. "He moves fast."

"He believes in really experiencing life."

"I don't blame him. It's why so many people come to these parties. To live."

"What about you?" Bethany asked. "Any family left?"

"My father. He's the guy who welcomes everyone to New Hope."

"He seems nice."

"That's part of his salesman pitch. He's got to really sell New Hope so we can keep the place running."

"I wouldn't think he'd have to sell anything. People want a place to be safe. They don't have to constantly watch over their shoulder here."

"They should."

"What do you mean?" Bethany asked.

"Nothing. Forget I said anything. Did your LSD kick in yet?"

"I don't know. I don't feel any different."

"Oh, you'll know when it does."

Bethany and Jennifer lapsed into silence, watching people dance and make out with each other. Bethany had never been to a high school party, but she imagined this was what one was like. As she watched the crowd, Bethany noticed a man shrouded in shadow watching her. While everyone else either faced the stage or was dancing, he was standing with his back to the stage staring at her. As she watched he approached her and Jennifer.

The man slit Jennifers throat and drew a nine on her forehead with her own blood. Bethany started screaming and turned and fled. She didn't want to watch anymore. She knew he would blood eagle her like the rest. She ran into the dark tunnel and tripped over the uneven floor. She fell onto her knees, but barely registered the cracking pain in her kneecaps. She crawled along the floor desperate to get back to the harsh artificial light of the town.

"Bethany!"

Her name echoed in the dark and bounced around her. She crawled against a wall and held her hands over her ears.

"Bethany!"

She trembled against the wall, her hands over her ears and looked around her frantically. She felt hands touching her and she screamed again.

"Shhh baby sister. It's Dean. Tell me what's wrong."

Bethany collapsed in his arms and sobbed. "He's here. He killed her. He's going to kill me."

"Shhh," Dean hushed again. "No one is dead honey. Did you take something at that party other than the drink Kevin gave you?"

Bethany sobbed into Dean's shirt. "I met a girl named Jennifer and she gave me some LSD and then he killed her and he's going to kill me. I'm number seven. I'm number seven."

"I'll go get Jennifer," Kevin said. "See if you can get her back to your room."

Bethany rocked back and forth on the ground. "I'm number seven." She mumbled over and over.

"Can you walk?" Dean asked as he stroked her hair. "Can you come with me back to our room. It's safe."

Bethany let Dean ease her from the cold ground and walked with his arm around her back toward the light. She kept mumbling 'I'm number seven,' as they walked back into the light.

"Do you want to go talk to the psychologist?"

Bethany shook her head vehemently. "I'm number seven. I'm number seven."

Dean managed to get Bethany back into their room and seated on her bed. She drew her legs up under her and just kept muttering about the number seven. A few minutes later there was a knock on the door and Dean let Kevin in. A girl came with him.

"This is Jennifer. She admitted she gave LSD to Bethany and when it kicked in Bethany stared at her in horror and started screaming and running. Do you want me to get Dr. Phil. Maybe he can help talk her down."

Dean ran his hands through his hair. "I don't know. I asked her about him, and she seemed even more freaked out. I don't want to add stress to the terrible trip she's already taking. When she comes out of it, I'll talk to him."

"Do you know what she's seeing?" Kevin asked.

"No. This is all my fault."

"Hey, no its not. All you did was encourage her to have some fun," Kevin said.

"But I told her I'd keep her safe. I knew she had some demons, but I didn't know how bad they were. I should have told her not to try LSD unless she was in a good mood. She's been on edge since she talked to the psychologist."

"Why don't you know what her demons are?" Jennifer asked. "You're her brother after all."

"She and I didn't meet until right before we were picked up by the convoy. We helped each other out of a situation and then we stuck together. She's just a kid so I told everyone she was my sister so we wouldn't get separated."

Dean sat down on the bed next to Bethany and took her hand while she stared at the wall and mumbled about being the number seven. Kevin sat down next to him and took his other hand.

"Despite how you came to be her brother, you're a damn good one."

"If you're done with me, I'm going back to the party," Jennifer said as she headed for the door.

The rest of the night Dean and Kevin watched over Bethany. Occasionally they offered her water, but she didn't move from her spot on the bed. When she finally came out of herself she cried again.

Dean hugged her. "I'm so sorry. . . can you tell me what you saw? Does it have to do with this?" Dean asked touching the seven on her forehead.

Bethany flinched. "Is Jennifer alright?"

"She's alive, just an idiot for giving you LSD and not asking what your mental state was beforehand."

"Beth, you kept saying he's going to kill me. Who is going to kill you? Did someone threaten you at the party?"

"No. I . . . I'm the seventh victim of the WYN killer."

"Oh honey, he's likely dead," Dean said as he held her hand. "He can't get you here."

"It's not even him anymore. Sometimes I wake up and I've done things to myself. She gestured at her arm and her forehead. That's why I need you to tie me up every night before I sleep."

"Did you tell the psychologist any of this?" Dean asked.

She sniffed. "Yes, but I don't want to talk to him. And I don't want anyone else to know. Please don't tell anyone."

"I mean I think the psychologist would be helpful, but that's your decision. I won't tell anyone else," Dean said.

"I won't either," Kevin said. "I'll go get some food for everyone and let you guys have a minute."

Dean and Bethany sat silent until Kevin was gone.

"What did you see last night?" Dean asked.

"The WYN killer. He slit Jennifers throat and wrote a nine on her forehead. He told me I was next." Bethany shook at the memory of what she had seen.

"How is she nine if you're seven?" Dean asked.

Bethany couldn't look at him while she answered. "I didn't just hurt myself."

"Are you telling me you murdered number eight?"

"I don't even remember doing it. One of the men in the group I was tentatively joining came and woke me up and showed me her body. Done just like the WYN killer did the other six. The same way he would have done me if he hadn't died."

"How do you know he's dead? Maybe he killed that girl."

"No, he would have killed me if he was still alive. It's been six months. And after all the other shit I've done to myself and didn't remember, I just know I killed Dutch too."

"Serial killers are fucked up babe. Maybe he did all these things to you and killed Dutch."

Bethany shivered. "I'd rather think I went insane rather than he's still alive. His death is the only thing keeping me from completely falling apart."

"I mean his death is plausible and highly probable."

Bethany knew Dean was humoring her, so she'd stop worrying and she appreciated it. She couldn't even think about WYN being alive. "Please don't tell Kevin. I'm sick over the things I've done."

"Honey, I don't believe you're capable of murder, but I'll keep your suspicions to myself."

Bethany wiped at her nose and gave him a grateful smile. He would never know how much she appreciated him. He was the best friend she'd ever had, and they'd only known each other for a week.

Kevin returned with food and the three of them ate in silence. Afterwords Kevin said his goodbyes and Dean got ready for work. He had the afternoon shift in the garden, which he'd excitedly told her did grow marijuana which he promised was a better high than LSD. A safer high. But for the moment Bethany was swearing off drugs. Her bad trip had perhaps ruined her party days.

After Dean left Bethany stared at the door from her bed. She knew she needed to leave the room, but leaving scared her. Her mind could just decide to snap at random. She sat in indecision until there was a knock at her door and she jumped. Hesitantly she got up and looked out the peephole before opening the door. Jennifer stood on the other side.

"Hey, sorry about your bad trip. What'd you start screaming for."

"I saw you get murdered."

"As if something like that could ever happen here," Jennifer said inspecting her nails. "Wana hang out?"

"Um . . ."

"Let's go weirdo," Jennifer said and started walking.

Bethany grabbed her key then followed Jennifer. She wasn't sure she wanted to continue hanging out with Jennifer, but they lived in a closed environment. She couldn't very well avoid her.

"Where are we going?" Bethany asked.

"The bowling alley. It's where people our age hang out."

Oh, great Bethany thought. People her age were cruel and judgmental. She'd rather not be exposed to them. Jennifer didn't join any of the groups of teenagers in the bowling alley though. She picked an empty lane and Bethany followed her.

"You don't hang out with the others?" Bethany asked. She'd taken Jennifer for a popular girl. One who had air for brains and the world handed to her.

"They don't hang out with me."

"Why?"

"Because I didn't have to fight and scrape my way here. My father worked here before the collapse. And when the dead started to rise, he moved us here. I haven't seen the sun in six months."

"Bummer. I miss the sun already and it's only been a day. And I know what its like to not have friends."

Jennifer shrugged and started the game. Bethany stayed and spent the rest of the day with her. She felt sorry for her after her admission that the other teens didn't hang out with her.

For the next several week Jennifer and Bethany were inseparable. They tried classes and apprenticeships. They swapped books and bowled together while Dean worked and grew closer to Kevin. And true to his word, Dean tied Bethany up every night before bed.

Life in new Hope was good. Better than her last few months before the fall. And Bethany began to think her dark past was behind her. She had friends. She had family. She had a budding life. The only problem was she had not stuck with any of her apprenticeships. Jennifer told her it was fine. Her father wouldn't kick Bethany out just because she hadn't found a job yet.

She was on her way to start a new one when she heard banging in the vent above her and her steps slowed. She looked up as she walked.

"What's your name," whispered out of the vent and she felt cold terror grip her chest as her feet stopped dead.

"What's your name?"

Bethany clapped her hands over her ears and tears rose unbidden to her eyes. She ran to the garden to find Dean. She banged on the glass that looked into the garden because non gardeners were not allowed inside. When he saw her face, he came out to meet her.

"What happened?" Dean asked.

"I heard a voice in the vent. And . . . and it asked me what my name was."

"Did you see anyone or hear anything else?"

She shook her head, still crying.

"Okay. I'm going to take you back to the room and make sure you're safe, then I'll tell your mentor that you're not coming to your apprenticeship."

Dean took Bethany back to their room and sat with her until she had calmed down. He pulled an edible from his drawer. They weren't allowed to smoke in the city, but the chemists distilled the marijuana and added it to food items.

"Eat some of this. It will help keep you calm. It's nothing like LSD so you don't need to worry about a bad trip. I'm going to see your mentor then I'll raincheck with Kevin."

Kevin and Dean had a special date night planned and Dean had been looking forward to it for weeks.

"No," Bethany said. "You go. I'll be fine in my room. If I start to freak out, I'll find Jennifer. Just make sure you make it back to tie me up before bed."

"Ok babe. Are you sure?"

"I don't want to ruin your date because I'm crazy."

"You're not crazy," Dean said then bent down and kissed her forehead. "You're the strongest person I know."

Dean left to see her mentor and she crawled under her covers and stared at the door. She knew no one could get in without a key, but it made her feel slightly better to watch the entrance to her room. Silent tears came back. She couldn't believe her paranoia had come back. Maybe she should have continued seeing the psychologist.

Roughly six months ago

Bethany sat on her bed staring at her window. She'd stopped going to school and talking to her parents. As time went on they'd begun to believe everyone else that she was lying. At first, they'd been angry at her. But then they began to smother her with attention thinking it would 'fix' her. All they'd done was alienate her. Her silence had freaked them out more and they'd forced her to see a psychologist who pumped her with medicine. She didn't think it was helping, but she took it to humor them. Behind her were the fading letters from the words 'what's your name'. She'd tried to scrub them off after she found them painted there when she woke up one morning. Another cry for help, she was told.

"What's your name?"

The whisper came from near her ceiling, and she looked up. There was nothing there.

"What's your name? What's your name? What's your name."

Bethany rolled over and held a pillow to her ears.

Present Day

Bethany's eyes fluttered open and she caught sight of the digital clock in her room. It was six am and she was untied, which meant Dean hadn't come home last night and done what he'd promised. Bethany checked herself for new marks but didn't find any. Next, she went to the bathroom and took a long hot shower. When she stepped from the tub, she noticed the writing in the steam on the window.

'What's your name?'

Her heart rate accelerated but she swiped it off. She didn't want to be a prisoner of her own mind again. She got dressed and left the room. She knew Dean was likely at Kevin's, so she wasn't worried about him. He was behind a locked door. She decided to go to the bowling alley and roll a few frames before going to find her mentor. Most people hadn't started the day yet. Body clocks did not work well underground. As Bethany stepped into the bowling alley, she noticed red splotches on the floor, and she stopped to stare at them.

Jim, the guy who ran the bowling alley would be pissed when he saw it. He ran a clean tight business. She stepped around and over the red spots. When she had made it past most of the mess she looked up once more and froze. Jennifers body was blood eagled and the words 'what's your name' had been written in her blood across the lanes.

Bethany's knees hit the ground and she screamed while she gouged at her own eyes. Jennifer had been her friend, but she'd noticed her blond hair when they met and knew she bore resemblance to a WYN victim. Now Bethany had killed her like she'd killed Dutch.

At some point while she was screaming and tearing at her face, she felt hands close around her arms and drag her away from the scene and locked in an office by herself. Her throat was raw, and her voice was hoarse from her screams. She rubbed at it trying to ease some of the pain. But there was no easing the pain in her heart. She'd killed one of the only friends she had.

A few minutes later Dean was ushered into the office, and he wrapped her in a hug. "What happened Bethany?"

She stood stiff in his arms. If he had come home last night this would never have happened. "I did it again. You broke your promise."

"I'm sorry I didn't make it home last night. But there is no way you did something. You were too distraught to leave the room."

"I killed Jennifer in the manner which was intended for me. My own friend."

"Shhh." Dean held his finger to her lips. "Don't say that too loud. They don't know what happened to Jennifer, let's just let them work while we devise a plan to get out of here."

"And go where? To kill again. Or to be lonely until I kill myself. Because I won't allow you to leave with me."

Jennifer's father walked in with tears in his eyes. He cleared his throat as he sat. "Please tell me anything you know about what happened to Jennifer."

"I killed her. It's not the first time I've done it. And I doubt it will be the last."

"Why?" he asked his shoulders sinking with the heavy knowledge his daughter's friend had killed her. "She adored you. You were the only person who was nice to her."

"I'm afraid I don't know. I don't remember these actions, but I can be certain it was me."

"She's talking crazy," Dean said, "Call Dr. Phil and let him evaluate her."

"It doesn't matter if she's insane or not. The punishment for killing a human is death by zombie."

"So, you're going to just turn her loose top side. Cause you'll be sending me too," Dean said.

The man shook his head. "We keep zombies on the lowest level for study."

"Think this over," Dean said. "She deserves a fair trial before you sentence her."

"There are no more judges and juries just the law of New Hope. And that law has been broken here tonight."

"Come Bethany," Jennifer's dad said.

Bethany followed him meekly. She was tired of fighting with herself. Of trying to remain sane. To be normal when she was broken beyond repair. Just like the Earth. Maybe the humans deserved what was happening to them, just as Bethany deserved to die for her sins.

Jennifer's dad led them below to a lab. Inside several cells were zombies. He positioned Bethany in front of the door to one. There was an airlock between the zombies and the door. She stepped inside and he shut the door behind her. When it was shut the door in front of her opened and she stepped into the cage with the zombies and waited for death. The zombies didn't register her presence at all unless you made a noise. And even then, they were easily distracted again.

"How are you doing this?" Jennifer's dad raged.

She shrugged. The zombies had never paid much attention to her. But they approached the glass at his yelling and started banging their heads into it trying to get to him. Bethny could see Dean and Jennifer's dad arguing, but she couldn't hear what they were saying over the zombies banging. Eventually Jennifer's dad pushed Dean out of the room, and she was left alone with the thudding until the silence calmed the zombies and they wandered aimlessly through the cell. Bethany sat down in a corner and pulled her knees up to her chin. Eventually maybe the zombies would find her and kill her. Until then she sat silently with her thoughts and wished the WYN killer had gotten her before the end of the world. At least two people would still be alive.

Time became meaningless in the glass case, and she was beginning to nod off when she heard voices again. Jennifers dad came back with Dean and Kevin.

"You've no right to hold my client," Kevin said.

Dean had told her Kevin was in law school when the apocalypse happened. And she knew he was probably only helping her out for Dean. She wanted to cry. Dean would not leave her here to be eaten or stand by while Jennifers dad killed her.

"I can't even believe I'm entertaining this farce. She admitted she killed Jennifer."

"I'm sure she'll recant her statement and without evidence you've got no case," Kevin said.

"Legalities are out the window. This is the god damned apocalypse. For fucks sake the dead walk."

"The law did not stop being the law because of the end of the world. And I'm sure the rest of your residents would like to know if they broke some sort of law in this town that they would receive a fair trial."

"She murdered my daughter," he said angrily.

"Did she?" Kevin rebutted. "Or maybe someone recognized her from before the world went to shit. And remembered she was the self-proclaimed seventh victim of the WYN killer and they decided to become a copycat and use her as a scapegoat."

"Jesus, just let her out. This punishment is a crime in itself. It's cruel and unusual," Dean said. "How can you justify letting her die like this?"

"Clearly, you've never lost a child. Anything that avenges her is justified."

"Think about this not as the victim's father, but as the leader of this community. The people need to see that if any one of them fucks up, they will get a fair trial," Kevin said.

"If you won't allow this punishment, I'll see she's banished," Jennifer's dad said as he opened the inside of the airlock.

Bethany moved into it and turned to make sure none of the zombies followed her. The inside door closed, and the outside door was opened. Hesitantly she stepped out. Jennifer's dad glared at her, but before he could say anything else, an alarm went off.

"What's that?" Dean asked.

"It means there are zombies loose in the city," Jennifer's dad said.

"How?"

"A new citizen was bitten and didn't tell anyone. A lab lost one. Who knows, now if you'll excuse me, I need to respond to this. Get her locked up."

Jennifer's dad left and Kevin hesitated before following him. Dean hugged Bethany.

"I'm so sorry," he said. "This is all my fault."

"No, it's mine. I should have never come down here. But I'm going to leave while he's distracted. You stay," she added as he started to open his mouth. "You need other people. And other people are safer away from me. I really appreciate you Dean. You're the best friend and older brother I've ever had. I hope you and Kevin are happy."

Dean hugged her again and sniffed back tears.

"You stay here until the danger passes. Stay safe."

"You too," Dean said.

Bethany left Dean there and headed back toward the upper levels. She hoped Jennifer's dad was right about just one zombie, but something felt off. There had to be precautions against something like this. As she made her way from floor to floor, she noticed there were bodies lying in the halls that looked like they had been mauled. She turned around to go back and get Dean. He was safer with her until they got out of the death trap of a city. Before she made it far something slammed into the back of her head, and she blacked out.

When she woke everything was dark, she couldn't move, and her body felt like ice. Something slid down her spine and she realized she wasn't dressed. Bethany shivered.

"What's your name?"

The whisper in her ear made her still as fear ate at her. She tried to tell herself it was all in her head, but this time the words rang hollow. She didn't recognize the voice, yet she did. She'd heard it whisper to her before.

"Oh, my dear how long I have waited for you."

Bethany shivered again. This time it wasn't in her head. The WYN killer had survived the apocalypse after all. "You've been stalking me for months and you still don't know my damn name?" The thought had just occurred to her and filled her with a smidge of anger. She was tired of living in fear.

He laughed. "I'm not asking what name your human form was given."

"What? What the fuck are you talking about?" She felt the sensation on her back again and realized he was stroking her spine.

"You are so much more than Bethany Clark seventeen-year-old girl. You are the seventh seal of Revelation, and I must open you to usher in the end of the end."

"Uh, nope just normal teenager here." In that moment she knew everyone who had said she wasn't pretty enough to be stalked by a serial killer had been wrong, and she'd wished they'd been right.

"And this is why I ask your name? You've forgotten who you are. As did all the others. But I will remind you one cut at a time, until you surrender yourself to it."

Bethany started crying. As sure as she had been she was ready to die just a little bit ago, she now found she wanted to live. Since he'd shown himself, she was certain he'd done all of the horrible things to her and other people she had been experiencing. "Why did you play with me? Why not just kill me."

"I must admit all of the theatrics were very entertaining. Even a god such as I enjoys a little levity."

The WYN killer slid a scalpel down Bethany's back, and she screamed. Unlike when he had killed victims eight and nine, this one felt right. She was the seventh seal. A fact that had been confirmed as he'd watched the zombies walk right by her without attempting to attack. They couldn't sense her like they sensed humans. She'd even lived with her zombie parents for several weeks before venturing out into the world. She had been close to starving and so had he. But he was not going to lose her by leaving the house for food. He'd almost opened her then, but it wasn't time. And then he'd gotten the idea to play with her a little. He'd gouged the tree and made it look like she'd done it with her fingernails. Then he'd cut her arm and forehead and murdered Dutch.

It hadn't been hard to join the caravan a couple days after her and blend into the new people so he could stay with her. He'd whispered out of the ducts and drew on her mirror and then he'd murdered her friend. All he'd had to do was wait until Dean forgot to tie her up.

"Pahplease don't," Bethany sobbed. "I don't want to die."

"You're not going to die, you're being opened into what your purpose is," he said as he sliced her flesh with a filet knife and peeled meat from bone. Bethany continued screaming until he started cutting her ribs and pulling them out of her back. He knew she was unconscious. They always went out about this part of the opening. His movements were smooth and precise as he finished her ribs and pulled her lungs out and laid them on her back. They were such beautiful wings. As he stepped back to admire his work Bethany began to turn. Her teeth clacked at him.

The WYN killer looked at her once more in admiration before walking out. The seals were all open and now it was time to remake the world.

Two-Bit Detective

Sunlight slanted through my broken shades and dappled across the ass of the latest undead who had come begging for my bed. Not because I was a good lay, but because I was a two-bit and we're rare. I lit up a cigarette and the smell roused her. She smacked it from my hand without looking.

"God those smell," she said, her voice muffled by the bed.

The one truly heinous thing about being undead was their heightened sense of smell and horrible smells made werewolves like my current bed partner irritable beyond belief. I patted her ass and lit another one as my phone rang. Answering it I moved to the kitchenette and started a pot of coffee. She followed me in a rage and began smashing things. I leaned against the counter with my arms crossed watching her amused while I listened to the phone call.

The call was from local PD. Seemed they had a crime scene for weird ol' me. I was a licensed PI and consult to the department on anything paranormal. And if they got an undead body, they handed the investigation to me. Humans simply did not care if the undead became all dead. And neither did I, but the pay rate was off the charts. Old money and all that.

I pulled on clothes, poured myself a coffee and left the still raging werewolf there. This happened every time I slept with a werewolf. Given their canine blood they had a tendency to get attached but they all hated the smell of cigarettes so the morning after I light one up. Drives them into a rage and they eventually leave after destroying my things. Luckily for me I lived around the corner from a thrift shop which made it easy and cheap to replace my shit. And I know what you're thinking. Why not just not fuck werewolves. And the answer to that is mind your own fucking business.

I hailed a cab and gave them the address to my crime scene. It's at a mausoleum in the middle of the oldest cemetery in town. He parks outside the police line and I get out. I smell something charred as I notice a freshly dug trench around the mausoleum. A couple of firefighters are in it. A makeshift bridge stretches over the trench, and I cross it. Inside

the mausoleum a circle of graveyard dirt surrounds a stone table. There's
a young girl lying on the table, eyes closed, black markings on her face.
her hands and feet are tied down and she's wearing a simple white gown.
She was something the undead might call a snack. Someone they'd love
to snap up and literally have for a snack.

"Thank god you made it Pete," a detective said when he noticed me.

My name is Randy but around the precinct I'm known as paranormal
Pete. "Looks like some kids playing at witchcraft. Why do you need me?"
The symbols on her face were unknown to me. And I'd known my share
of witches. But what else could it be?

All of a sudden, the girl sat up and jerked against her ropes. A growl
rolled out of her throat and her eyes were inky black as she looked at us.

"Oh shit," I said. "Get me the Harlots."

The Harlots for the Lord were an undead gospel group, and I often
consulted them on cases. They were radical in their love and belief in the
lord. So much so they weren't above killing for him.

"Any idea who the girl is or whose grave this is?" I asked.

"Some poor unfortunate soul," the detective said.

The detective stepped out of the mausoleum, and I circled the slab.
The girl relaxed back in the stone and went back to looking like she was
dead. On the inside of her elbows was another symbol. Her bare feet
were stained black with what I assumed was ink. Her body rose back off
the slab and a scream ripped from her throat as I inspected her. Her body
hung in the air, her ankles and wrists straining against the ropes.

"You do not contact the girls directly. You know this, Randy. All
communication goes through- sweet Mary and Joseph what is that?"

I turned to look at the Harlots Jesus centric manager, Keith. He was
dressed in a track suit with the words JESUS SAVES printed on the back
of the jacket.

"I called the holy trinity because I wanted them, not you Keith.
What the fuck can you do with this?" I asked as I gestured at the girl who
floated back down to the slab and closed her black eyes.

"I'm responsible for them," Keith said.

I laughed. "Responsible for finding them lunch."

The three Harlots walked in one at a time, dressed in their typical nun attire. I stepped back and let them take in the room. They glided across the space. One sank to her knees and sniffed the dirt.

"Any idea which demon is stuck inside of her and why?" I asked.

While I was alright at the paranormal, I still had a lot to learn about the religious. My parents had both been atheist and never sent me to church. Given my line of work, I'm a believer in a great many things though organized religion is not one.

"Not a demon."

"Something older."

"Can we get it out of her?" I wasn't going to add the word safely. The girl had a dagger in her chest for Christ's sake.

"You've stumped us dear Pete. Call a witch to lock this mausoleum while we do some research."

The nuns continued to circle the altar while I called the only witch I had ever met. Kazm belonged to the largest and oldest coven in town, and I'd met her on a case. Like the Harlots she was a consultant I called in from time to time. She breezed into the crime scene, hair and robes flowing behind her like a god damned dream. I was lost in her entrance until I heard the harlots hissing at her.

I spun and snapped at them. "Play nice zealots. it was you who told me to call a witch."

I should have known this would happen. I mean they did have a song called burn witch burn. Kazm ignored them even when they started spitting in her direction and breezed over to me.

"What do you need Randy?" Kazm asked.

I pointed at the body, my mouth suddenly dry.

She smiled. "I think you need a necromancer."

The girl sat up and screamed.

"Oh, I see. She's got a darkling in her. But you didn't need me to tell you that. The harlots could have."

I looked over at the three of them grinning, their fangs showing. "Okaay. They said they wanted you to lock up this tomb while they did research."

"They do need me to lock this tomb, but if I had to guess they were going to hunt the bastard that did this," Kazm said.

"Huh," I said as I lit a cigarette. The harlots immediately left the tomb and Jesus centric Keith went with them. "Is there any way to get it out of her?"

Kazm moved to stand behind her head. The girl tilted her face back to stare at her. Kazm stroked the girl's hair. "No." She bent over the girl's face and gripped both sides of her head then began to whisper words over her. The girls eyes slipped closed and Kazm stood up.

"Did you just . . . kill her again?"

"No. I put the creature inside of her to rest. The marks have bound it inside her."

"Now what?"

"Now I seal the tomb and you try to find a family to contact and let them know she isn't coming home."

"On the upside they don't have to pay for the burial," I said as I turned to leave. I knew the tomb was in her capable hands and I could really use another cup of coffee. By now my secretary Ada would have one sitting on my desk ready for me.

The super N detective agency sat nestled between two empty and crumbling store fronts. An apt appearance for the shit I dealt with. The inside didn't look any better though it was a sight cleaner. Ada refused to work in filth she said and so she was very diligent with cleaning the two rooms that made up our little office. Her desk faced the door in the outer room which looked pleasant, a word I acquainted with Ada herself. She was always put together and had a demeanor that invited clients in. Her room had a nice soft paint and she kept beautiful pictures on the walls and her desk. My office sitting directly behind hers was, however, plain. Like myself. I didn't want anything about my appearance or office to tell anyone too much about me. It was a good way for work to follow you home. I did, however, embellish my plain suits with a detective style hat. All good detectives must have a hat that denotes their title.

When I entered Ada sat at her desk, the telephone to her ear. I presumed it was another haunted house call. Despite how exciting my morning had been, most of my cases were haunted homes. I spent a great deal of time finding out what ghost was haunting what and arranging cleansings. As I passed her, I motioned her to come to my office when she was done with her call. As I suspected, a fresh cup of coffee sat on my desk and I sat to enjoy it until she came in. Breathing in the smell I let my eyes slide closed and I listened to Ada's soft tones in the other room.

I opened my eyes when I heard the phone click into its cradle. Ada breezed into the room with her own coffee in hand.

"You got a case?" I asked as she sat.

"If you handled standard human runaways then yes. But seeing as this is the Super N agency, No."

Also by Eady H

Double Creature Feature
Double Creature Feature

Valoryn Universe
The End of Creation Enforcement

Standalone
The Earth Swallows
Where the Dark Things Are
Two-Bit Detective
Boken Girl Broken World